# WUTARYOO

By NILAH MAGRUDER

**Versify**
Houghton Mifflin Harcourt
Boston   New York

Versify® is an imprint of Houghton Mifflin Harcourt Publishing Company. Versify is a registered trademark of Houghton Mifflin Harcourt Publishing Company.

hmhbooks.com

The illustrations in this book were done digitally.
The text was set in Tyke ITC Std.
Cover design by Andrea Miller
Interior design by Andrea Miller

Library of Congress Cataloging-in-Publication Data
Names: Magruder, Nilah, author, illustrator.
Title: Wutaryoo / by Nilah Magruder.
Description: Boston : Houghton Mifflin Harcourt, [2022] | Audience: Ages 4 to 7. | Audience: Grades K–1. | Summary: Wutaryoo enjoys hearing other animals' origin stories but wants to learn her own, so she sets out on a journey on which she meets many strange creatures and learns important truths.
Identifiers: LCCN 2019047580 (print) | LCCN 2019047581 (ebook) | ISBN 9780358172383 (hardcover) | ISBN 9780358172369 (ebook)
Subjects: CYAC: Identity—Fiction. | Animals—Fiction. | Voyages and travels—Fiction.
Classification: LCC PZ7.1.M346 Wut 2021  (print) | LCC PZ7.1.M346  (ebook) | DDC [E]—dc23
LC record available at https://lccn.loc.gov/2019047580
LC ebook record available at https://lccn.loc.gov/2019047581

Manufactured in China
SCP 10 9 8 7 6 5 4 3 2 1
4500833403

To my father, and all the other stories that never got told

To my cousins, nieces, and nephews, and all the other
stories waiting to be heard

She was called Wutaryoo, and she lived there, in that shallow hole in the earth.

She was the only one, and she did not know

She did not know her name either,
but now and then a creature would
come upon her and say,

Wutaryoo did not know how to answer this question—so she would ask it back.

And the creatures would tell their tales.

"What am I? I am the rabbit.
In the beginning, the first gardener
was digging a hole to plant his cabbages.

"He dug too deep and hit the very
center of the world, and you know
what popped out? Rabbits!

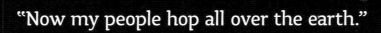

"Now my people hop all over the earth."

*Wow,* thought Wutaryoo.

"What am I? I am the wren, queen of the hedge!
In the beginning, my people were as large
as trees and ruled the world.

"Our size has grown smaller,
but not our might!"

*Magnificent*, thought Wutaryoo.

"What am I? I am the wolf. In the beginning, my people were born in moonlight. Now we run and hunt together, and at night, we sing our thanks to the heavens."

*Wondrous*, thought Wutaryoo.

What would be more wondrous, though, was if Wutaryoo could share her own story.

Every day, creatures large and small
regaled her with their tales.

The bullfrog,

the fox,

the elephant,

the honeybee,

the tortoise,

and, finally, the great whale,
oldest and wisest of them all.

One night, Wutaryoo looked up to the moon.

"What am I?
Who are my people?
Where did I come from?
Surely, I have a story, too."

But the moon did not know either.

The next morning, Wutaryoo started walking and did not stop.

Her friends had all come from someplace else. If Wutaryoo could find where she came from, maybe her story would be waiting there.

"I will search far and wide," she said to herself.
"I will go all the way to the very beginning of
the world if I have to."

Wutaryoo journeyed under tall trees, through dense grass, and over rolling hills.

She walked until she could walk no more.

So, she swam. On strange shores, she found
a creature she had never seen before.

"I am the dodo. I have seen many suns
rise and set over these islands,
but I have never seen a creature
like you. What is your story?"

"I don't know," said Wutaryoo.
"But I will soon."

Wataryoo continued on, over rising terrain,
until she reached mountains too tall to climb.

So, she dug.
Deep in the earth, she found
a creature she had never seen before.

"I am called the dragon, the terrible lizard,
and many other names. My bones are
spread far and wide through this earth,
but I have never seen a creature like you.
What is your story?"

"I don't know," said Wutaryoo.

"But I will very soon."

Wutaryoo continued on, deep and deeper and deeper still,
until it was so dark she could no longer see

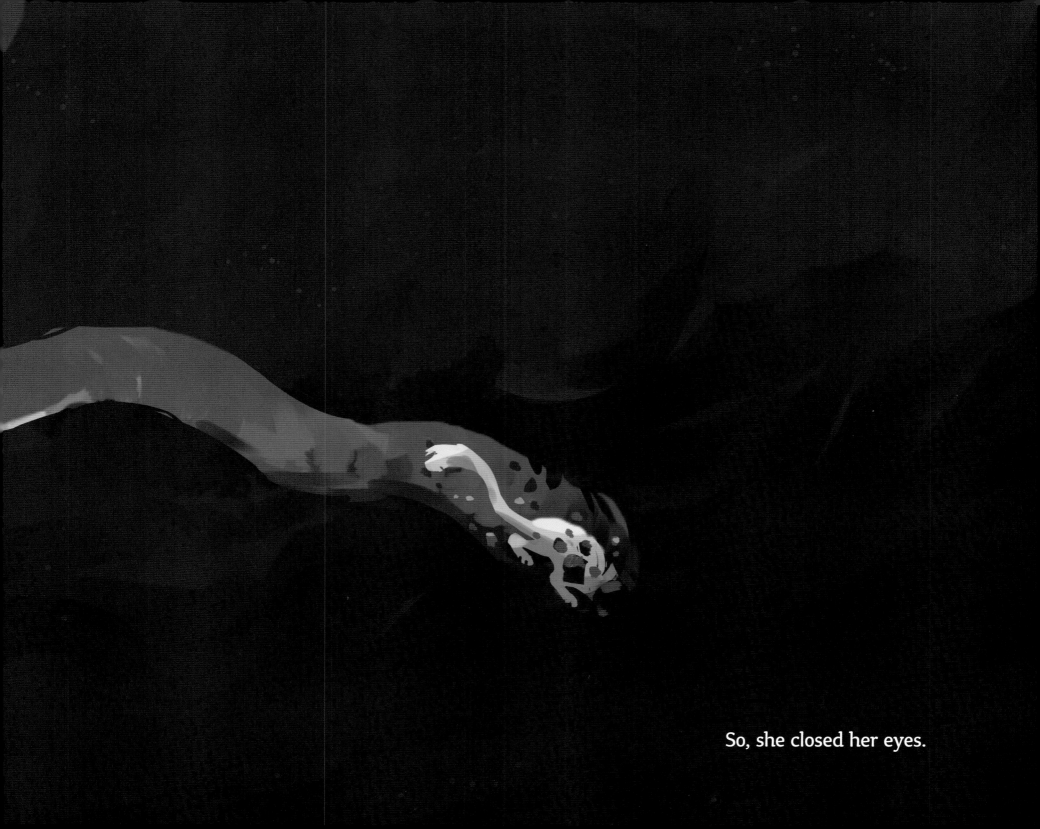

So, she closed her eyes.

When she opened them, there was a tiny, very tiny light.

She crawled toward it and found
a creature she had never seen before.

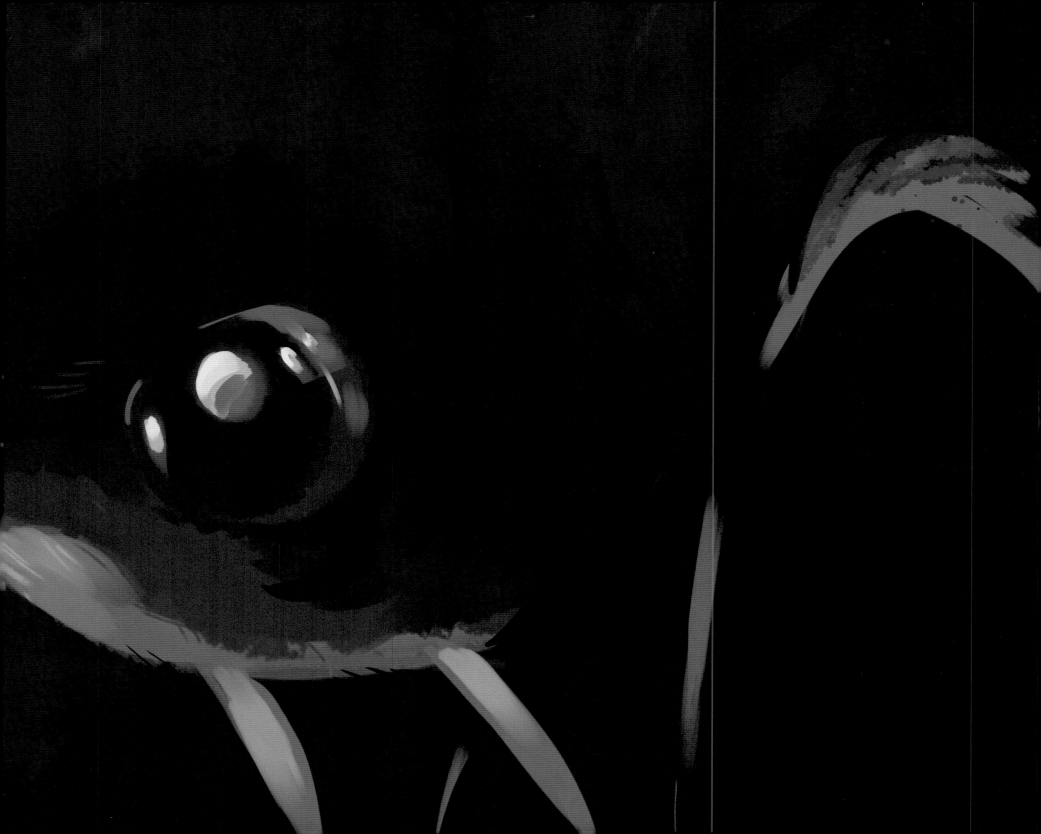

"I am the protozoan," it said to her.

"I have been here since the beginning.
I have seen it all, more than I can ever tell,
but I have not seen a creature like you."

"Oh," said Wutaryoo.

"You have come a long way to find me. Tell me,
have you discovered what you are searching for?"

"Not yet. But I think I'm getting close now."

Wutaryoo walked farther than she had ever walked,
and the land grew sparser than it had ever grown.

*I am coming to the very beginning of the world, she thought.*
*My story must be over that last hill.*

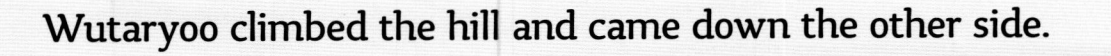

Wutaryoo climbed the hill and came down the other side.

But there was no story there.
All Wutaryoo found . . . was a shallow hole.

Her shallow hole.

She had come right back to where she had started.

Sad, and tired, Wutaryoo curled up.

Just as she was falling asleep, she heard her name.

Her friends surrounded her.
*Here it is*, thought Wutaryoo,
*the same old question.*

They will ask her what she is,
and she will have to confess,

"I don't know.

I don't know what I am,
or where I come from.

Perhaps I come from nowhere.

Perhaps I am nothing."

But before she could say these things,
her friends asked questions Wutaryoo
had not heard before.

"Are you all right?"

"Where did you go?"

"What did you see?"

"What did you hear?"

For none of them had traveled
as far or as long as Wutaryoo.

So, Wutaryoo told them about her adventures:

how far she had walked,
swam, dug, and crawled;

about the creatures
she had met—strange,
terrible, and wonderful;

and how her long journey,

over hills, across oceans,
and under mountains,

had finally brought her home.

At the end, her friends were
very quiet, taking it all in.

Then the whale, oldest and wisest of them all, said,
"Now, Wutaryoo. That is a wondrous story, indeed."

The creatures nodded. "Tell it again."

And Wutaryoo did.

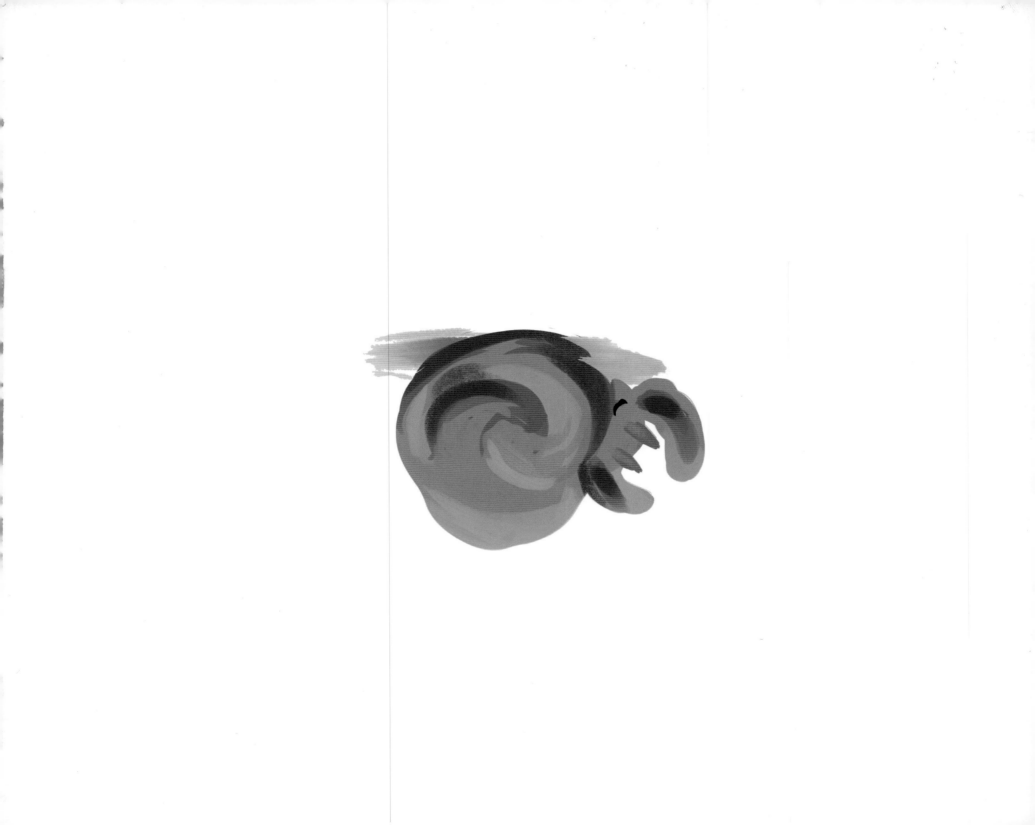